The Curator

By

Sean De Siun

imaginative fiction

Published October 2015
by Fileata Fiction.

This is the first in a series of short novels, Moral Tales.

Cover: *After the Bath* Degas, *Maternity* Picasso, *Bathers at Asnière* Seurat, *The
Toilet of Venus* Velasquez, *Bacchus and Ariadne* Titian
Back cover: *Flowers with Fish* Sean De Siun.

This book is a work of fiction any resemblance to events or
people past or present is absolutely amazing, but is wholly
a product of the author's imagination.

A CIP record for this book is available
from National LIbrary of Australia

ISBN 978-0-9806049-8-6

COPY SALES
The Curator is available on **www.amazon.com**
Purchase direct from **www.fileata.com**

Distribution enquiries:
Fileata Fiction
PO Box 246
Edgecliff NSW 2027
Australia

ISBN 978-0-9806049-8-6

9 780980 604986 >

imaginative fiction

1

Louis awoke to the sound of his young baby crying as Sandrine walked through the open bedroom door from the bathroom to the baby's cot, 'Petite Julie, calme-toi.

She picked the baby up in her arms and gently rocked her back and forth. Sitting on the end of the bed she opened her white blouse and put the baby to her breast. The composition and the haunting beauty of Sandrine reminded him of the Picasso painting, *Maternity,* from 1909.

Louis sat up in bed and admired the beautiful scene. As in the painting, Sandrine was so absorbed in feeding her child that the rest of the world seemed not to exist for her. Like a statue come to life, her small tender movements and serene smile evoked the universal image of motherhood.

How lucky he was, he thought. Sandrine looks so happy. She was at that very moment, the image of perfection. The room was warm and filled with the soft clinging smell of new birth. The only sound was the whispered sucking of the baby on Sandrine's full breast.

Sandrine was actually not that young a mother. Louis remembered the night they had met, nearly twelve years earlier. He smiled to himself; she looks even more beautiful now than she did then. She was ten years younger than Louis. They met in Paris and were married two years later, but baby Julie had been her first pregnancy. How time flies, he thought. What happened to those years? Still, no matter, here we are, a proper family at last.

Sandrine looked up at Louis and laughed softly, 'You had better make your own breakfast cheri.'

He padded downstairs in his socks made toast and porridge. Soon Sandrine came into the kitchen and said, 'The baby is asleep now.'

www.pablopicasso.org/maternity.jsp

Louis watched her as she picked up his empty plates from the table, turned and took them to the sink. She was self-assured, her eyes bright and loving. He admired her hands and her behind as she turned her back. He felt a stirring and remembered the feeling of pressing his fingers around her curves.

He loved her, but why her? Of all the women he had met before Sandrine, of all the women he encountered day by, why was it she, in particular, that had taken his love? What was her unique beauty that captured him? He seemed to have forgotten. All he could perceive was feminine, maternal beauty, not Sandrine's uniqueness.

'I'm off now my love,' he said rising from his chair.

Louis took the tube to work. He liked to read on the train and enjoyed the distraction of being embroiled in a story. But more importantly he sought the anonymity that hiding behind a book cover gave him. No one in the carriage paid the least attention to him while they assumed he was reading. He could observe the people unnoticed and a woman somewhere in the carriage would always grab his attention.

This morning it was a young dark haired woman opposite him. She looked at her phone absorbed. Now bored, with no new messages, she put her phone in her handbag and gazed up at the ceiling, lost in some other world.

Louis peered out over the top of his book, trying to decide about her. No longer so quick to classify the women he saw as ones that he would like to be with or not. He took his time to consider whether they possessed the indefinable quality, that something that a woman had to have to attract him. His blood was not so quick to rush and fill him with desire as it used to be. Married, aging, he was just a passive observer.

The beauty of women and the allure of sex filled his mind. The intoxicating mixture of anticipation and uncertainty tore at his heart. I'm just same as everyone else in that regard, he thought. But it was a woman's face, expression and gestures that interested him. He imagined that in these stolen moments he witnessed their intimate inner thoughts. That the mystery of their essence was being revealed to him, conveyed through subtle movements, a smile or frown, the smallest things.

The dark haired woman stood up and moved towards the doors. The train came to a sliding stop at Victoria and she disappeared into the crowd. What if I had met this woman before Sandrine? Would I have fallen in love with her, wanted to have a child with her? The constant yet fleeting presence of women I will never see again. Is it enough that I feel their charm without giving in to it? I feel life passing me by and frustrated not to have held each one of these women even for an instant.

The train arrived at Charring Cross and the doors of the carriage burst open with a hiss. With the madding crowd, he trundled out the doors, up the stairs, along the never-ending corridor and past the buskers. He felt like a fish in a giant school, turning with all the others gaping, swimming to and fro. Being in a crowded street or train was a tonic for him. It brought him peace and his best ideas came to him while he flowed through the stream of people. Eventually, he made his way out into the street and walked across Trafalgar Square to the National Gallery where he worked.

Louis was a Curator and enjoyed his role. He had joined the Gallery before he met Sandrine and had made his way up the echelons gaining his Masters Degree and publishing various treatises along the way. Now he was in a senior position and his career was set. One day he may even be appointed the head of Curation. His life was solid, stable, built on sound foundations, and he thought it would stay that way.

He nodded good morning to the gallery staff as he made his way up to his office. He walked with a slight swagger, his left hand in his suit jacket pocket. He affected a reserved, but friendly demeanour. He had been brought up to understand the importance of projecting an appropriate air.

The lift door opened on his level and he said good morning to lovely Emily, the receptionist. She was definitely to his taste and had that certain something. But he was sure not to let his impure thoughts be noticed by anyone. No, he just admired the beauty of women. That was all. After all I do work in the arts, he assured himself.

Although he sometimes imagined how it would be to embrace and kiss the women he observed, he had not had an affair with anyone since he moved in with Sandrine, one year after they had first met. He would remain faithful, of course, until ... until the baby grows up at least. I have that responsibility now. I can't let my family down. Then I'll be an old man in any case.

Louis met Sandrine on a working visit to Paris where she was employed at the Musée d'Orsay. A year later she moved from Paris to London. The next year they married and bought their apartment at Bayswater. Although he was brought up in London, Louis' mother was from Paris and he had spent much time there. He had attended the Lycée Français in London and spoke fluent French. Indeed, being bi-lingual had been a great boost to his career.

That day he had a lunch appointment with an old friend called David. One o'clock arrived and he made his way to the National Dining Rooms in the Sainsbury Wing. The lift doors swished open and he went out into the never-ending stream of people.

There were thousands of people of all shapes, sizes and nationalities jabbering in a multitude of languages. Like a lion looking at a herd of zebra, they melded together in a jumble of colour and shape. Until his eyes picked out an individual, a woman gazing at a painting lost in thought, or reading on a bench.

He breezed along the corridor to the restaurant nodding to the staff along the way. David was waiting for him sitting at a table by a window looking out onto Trafalgar Square. 'Louis, how are the baby and Sandrine?'

'They are both very well. Sandrine is in a state of bliss, and the baby sleeps most of the time.'

David had attended the same university as Louis although he was a bit older than him. After a while their conversation slowed and they both sat in silence.

David noticed Louis' head turning from left to right as he watched passers by in the street below. 'Stop undressing the girls as they walk by Louis,' he said.

'I'm not, I'm only looking, looking at their eyes, and their faces.'

'Why are you looking at all Louis? You have a beautiful wife at home.'

'A cat can look at a queen they say. Nothing wrong with looking, you know that's all I ever do,' said Louis.

'You're doing a bit more than looking in your mind. It's still a sin,' David laughed.

'Really? You think it wrong of me? I am a red blooded man. I can't help it if there are beautiful women around. What am I supposed to do, close my eyes?'

'Avert your eyes Louis. Avert your eyes and don't be so obvious.'

'Am I that obvious? Maybe it's just because you know me. I never see a woman look back at me, never.'

'Ah, maybe they're averting their eyes. Perhaps they are more polite than you.'

'Women are never attracted to me. In all these years I have never had an affair, unlike you David. If there is one thing I am incapable of now, it's flirting with a girl. I have no idea what to say and no reason to speak to her,' said Louis.

'Yes well, at least I'm honest with myself. I like women and sometimes they are attracted to me. I don't pretend to be disinterested like you do. Then sometimes, you know, one thing leads to another. A glance, chemistry, the brush of hands, that's how men and women get together. It just happens.'

'You're as married as I am David. Besides, what do you mean I'm disinterested?'

'I've seen it many times over the years. You eye up a girl, she looks back at you and you turn away. I've seen several girls become attracted to you, even approach you. But you always act is if you don't like them and brush them away.'

'Have I done that? I can't believe it. Who was attracted to me?'

'Lucinda is one example. Remember her a couple of years ago? You really missed out there. She's married now. But you only want to look, not actually make love. Isn't that right?'

'It's true, I sometimes feel that marriage closes me in and I want to escape. I miss the time when I could experience the pang of anticipation. But I avoid situations where I might get entangled with other women. I rarely go to parties; I don't go to clubs looking for women. I don't chase women full stop. That doesn't mean I don't desire something more. But you do all those things. You go out with your colleagues to clubs, leave your wife at home and look for girls. Of course sometimes you find one.'

'Louis, I'm mostly faithful to my wife although I may deceive her now and then, but you're wrong. I don't go hunting for women. I go out for entertainment, a good time with my friends. I don't look for it, but I don't refuse it either. I let nature take its course. The women I've known are real people, flesh and blood. Life isn't planned, laid out like a perfect composition. Occasionally something happens and I meet someone. It seems to me that your way is detached, cold. You pretend you're faithful, but cheat in your mind ten times a day.'

Louis had no answer to David's disturbing observations. He stared once again out into the square with nothing to say. Am I really so transparent, such a hypocrite?

David interrupted Louis' soul searching, 'Cheer up old boy. Don't take me so seriously. I was only ribbing you. Speaking of parties, you know it's my 50th birthday in June don't you?'

'Yes of course I remember. How are you going to celebrate it?'

'We'll go to the country house for the weekend. I'm inviting a bunch of friends, old and new, for a house party. You must come, bring the family.'

'In June the baby will only be four months old. I don't think we'll be able to make it.'

'I know, but I can't move the date of my birthday. You're invited, remember that. Come by yourself. Maybe by then you and Sandrine will be ready for a break. Having a new baby puts a lot of pressure on couples, believe me. It might be healthy for you to leave them alone for a day or two. Keep it in mind anyway.'

2

Louis soon forgot his conversation with David. Family life took over and the weeks sped by. David had been right about the pressure on him and Sandrine. The baby no longer slept through the night and he was tired and ragged. Sandrine encouraged him to go. 'Cheri it's just for the weekend and don't worry about us. You need a break. Besides, David is your oldest friend and it's his 50th.'

On Saturday afternoon he drove down the A40 to the house at Chalfont St Giles.

Sandrine kissed him, 'Au revoir cheri, see you Monday.'

He felt light hearted as he drove. He had no expectations for the weekend, save to get a little bit drunk and have a good time. He remembered his conversation with David and thought he had been unfair. He had been faithful to Sandrine, not just in body. Being married suited him. He was happier not having to worry about relationships with women. He could pursue his interests without the pressure of having to find a girlfriend.

When he first met Sandrine they were attracted to each other straight away. He asked her out to dinner. Perhaps it was just that he was an Englishman who could actually speak French, but she enjoyed his company. She smiled and looked at him amorously, held his hand and moved closer to him. Her big green eyes stared into his.

Louis returned to London after a short while, but they kept up their relationship long distance. He regularly went to Paris for weekends and Sandrine came to London often as well. It was not exactly a hardship for either of them as Louis loved Paris and Sandrine London.

Sandrine worked in administration but was ambitious and determined to pursue a career in arts centre management. Louis knew many people in the arts scene in London and was quite socially active in those days. It soon became apparent that having Sandrine at his side at dinner parties and functions was advantageous. It seemed to transform him from a boring academic into an exotic art historian. He could hold forth and people would listen, even if they were only there to be in the orbit of Sandrine. She made him seem more stable, substantial. Having a beautiful, young French girlfriend who worked at the d'Orsay impressed his superiors at the Gallery no end. He was good for Sandrine's career for the same reasons. In Paris, they seemed to fit into the arts clique seamlessly.

It could easily have happened the other way around, but it was through a contact of Louis' that Sandrine heard about a position at the National Portrait Gallery and she moved to London and in with him.

Everything seemed to fit together so well. They were a perfect match so everyone said, including his mother. 'Don't let her get away Louis, you'll never find better than belle Sandrine,' she said.

Of course, Louis had been in relationships before. He had broken up with Hillary not long after meeting Sandrine. Actually she had left him. She said he was too self-centered. All his previous relationships seemed to end up the same way. None were satisfying not even with Zoe, who had gone out with for years. He put it down to the constant studying and research that he had to do to further his budding career. So it seemed that marrying Sandrine was the natural thing to do.

As Sandrine was younger than Louis, she wanted to wait to have children and pursue her career. For years, they had been so wrapped up in their work that they spent less and less time with each other. Every now and then he would hear whispers or snide remarks about his too perfect relationship with his too beautiful and too young trophy wife. But that was the way it was in London and Paris for that matter. People could be vicious, jealous.

The years sped by and eventually Sandrine was ready to have a child. Now Louis rather late in life was a father. He looked back at his relationship with Sandrine with affection. They were fond of each other; they had been good for each other and had stayed together despite everything.

Louis pulled into the driveway of David's country mansion in the Chilterns just outside London. He hadn't asked David who else would be there. What did it matter anyway? It would be a couple of days with no responsibilities, and he was sure there would be no women for him to admire. It would just be the usual crew of aging, married friends of David.

David ran a hedge fund and he was rich. Not exactly a boy, but even after all the years Louis had known him, he still behaved like one. Caterers had been arranged for the weekend with no expense spared, so David had promised.

He pulled into the long driveway and parked. As he opened his car door, he heard laughter and clinking of glasses. He made his way up the steps and into the vestibule to be greeted by a waiter and took a glass of champagne. He found an empty chair in the living room and sat down. It was mostly the usual group of old friends, but there were some new faces as well. A friend of David's from their university days sat to his left. Crashing old bore thought Louis. On his right was David's wife Anna who was always charming and talkative.

Contented, detached, he nibbled hors d'oeuvres and sipped his drink without joining in the conversation. Across the room a couple he had not encountered before introduced themselves to those around them. The man was dark and a bit sombre. He spoke softly, his eyes looking downward as if embarrassed. Occasionally he became more animated and strident. He referred to his partner as 'darling Agata.'

Agata certainly is a darling thought Louis. It was not that she was particularly good looking. She had a wide face with a strong jaw and a slender figure. She moved her hands animatedly. Wearing a moderately low cut top, her breasts moved pleasantly when she laughed. As she spoke earnestly, on import and learned subjects her blond hair danced around her shoulders. She had a strange accent hard to place that only increased her allure. But it was her eyes that were her best feature, blue, large and sparkling.

Agata looked Louis in the eye when speaking in his direction. Surprised, he moved his hand to cover his chin, is she talking to me? He now felt obliged to enter the conversation and made an attempt to be charming. Certain he had failed to impress her, he redoubled his efforts. Several times she looked him straight in the eye and asked him poignant questions about art and politics. He was fascinated by her, but she was taken, or so it seemed.

Later on, Louis was drinking with several of the men in David's study. Undertones of machismo and bawdiness came to the fore as the men became increasingly intoxicated. David, his eyes reddened by the alcohol, asked Agata's partner, 'So what's she like Mark, you know, between the sheets?'

'She's not my girlfriend David,' he replied.

The men faces distorted in drunkenness winked at each other. 'I'll bet she's a tiger Mark eh? Go on you can tell us,' urged David to peels of laughter. But he received no further response from Mark, who looked sheepishly into his drink.

Not his girlfriend? So what is, 'darling Agata' to Mark? Louis wondered.

Dinner was to be served and Louis took a random seat at the long table in the richly decorated dining room. The chair next him was empty and as if from nowhere, Agata appeared and sat down.

'Louis, I'm so glad you came for the weekend. I've met several of David's friends now but you're the most interesting so far,' she said, her eyes looking straight into his.

He nearly fell out of his seat. It was not her sudden appearance that shook him. No, he was astonished that she was interested in him at all, yet there were her big blue eyes, piercing him as if straight into his soul.

She cannot be interested in me, he thought. It's just the first time in years that I'm having a real conversation with a woman, that's all. Normally it is just polite, distant chit chat. I'm not used to someone like Agata talking to me in this way. She is just trying to be friendly, nothing more.

'Agata, that's nice. I'm glad to meet you as well. But tell me, where are you from? You have such an exotic accent.'

'I'm from Poland Louis, although I haven't lived there for years.'

Ah, Poland, that might explain it he thought. She is so much more direct than the English women I work with and meet at gallery openings and formal occasions.

'How long have you been in London?'

'It's been nearly a year already. I was in the USA for many years, studying and working before coming here.'

'I guess that's why your accent is so different.'

'Yes, I mostly learned English in America.'

He thought it impolite to ask her age, but he judged her to be in her early thirties. 'What do you do Agata, for a living?'

'I'm a physicist'

'You must have spent many years studying?'

'Yes, it's true I have Physics and Computer Science degrees. My PhD took a lot of effort, but I enjoyed it. How about yourself, what did you study Louis?'

'Me, nothing really, you know, Art History. I just looked at pictures in books and went to museums.'

Mark sat down across the table from Louis. 'I think I had a one too many G&Ts darling Agata,' he said looking at the two of them. He turned his face to look directly at Louis, smiled and lowered his eyes.

'Well Mark go easy on the wine with dinner eh? We have to get up early in the morning for the croquet game.'

'Yes darling, don't worry about me,' he murmured without raising his eyes.

Soon the dining room was filled with guests grabbing chairs and engaging in lively conversation. Agata was very popular; everyone wanted to talk to her. Giles, seated at the far end, shouted down the length of the table in an upper-class accent with everyone forced to listen in. She had a dry sense of humour and laughter reverberated around the table at her jokes. Louis was disappointed. He had barely spoken to her at all and now he was just one small voice butting into the discussion. He gave up trying to impress her and faded into the background.

David had an exceptional wine cellar and the waiter diligently refilled Louis' glass as soon as it was half empty. Louis was enjoying himself now, lost in a drunken internal debate about the merits of the wines that had been served. He was sure he glimpsed Agata looking at him out of the corner of her eye several times even though she wasn't talking to him.

After dinner, brandy was served. Louis swished his glass around and took his first sip. um, excellent Armagnac. Looking up he caught Agata in a full on stare. Her eyes danced away from his, embarrassed at having been caught admiring him. Mark was deeply engrossed in a conversation with the crashing bore while Anna, who had swapped places and was now sitting opposite, smiled knowingly at Agata and Louis.

Recomposed, Agata asked, 'What part of town do you live in Louis?"

'Bayswater, you know, on the north side of Kensington Gardens.'

'Oh, not far from the Serpentine Gallery?'

'No, not far at all.'

'There's an exhibition on there at the moment that I would like to see. I was thinking of going during the week.'

My God thought Louis, she wants me to take her. 'Really, what's the exhibition? I should know of course in my line of work, but I don't recall what's on there at the moment.'

'Yes Louis, you work at the National Gallery don't you?' asked Agata tilting her head to one side as if genuinely curious.

Anna didn't let Louis reply and butted in, 'Agata, I would love to go the Serpentine gallery, I haven't been there in ages. How about we go together?'

'Anna, yes, thanks, that would be lovely.'

'Wonderful, I'll call you on Monday and arrange it. I can't wait.'

Anna looked at Louis triumphant that she had foiled his chance of a tryst with Agata. Mark finished his conversation with the crashing bore as David slapped Louis on the shoulder and declared, 'Everyone, time to take our brandies out to the veranda.'

Louis lingered at the table hoping to be left alone with Agata as everyone left, but Anna whisked her away gushing, 'Agata, I have something wonderful to show you, come with me.'

He stayed as if stuck to his chair while he struggled to make sense of what had just happened. I know I'm a bit tipsy, but I 'm sure Agata wants to see me, alone, away from Mark. I know that look, those glances. I may have been married for years, but I still remember how a girl looks at you when she wants you. Maybe I'm wrong, perhaps she's just flirtatious. But I'm going to find out one way or the other.

Determined, he stood up straight, pushed his fingers through his hair. He placed his left hand in his jacket pocket and with the best slight swagger he could muster, followed the boisterous party out into the late evening air.

After one o'clock Agata and Mark said goodnight and went upstairs to bed. Louis followed soon after; there was no point staying up if Agata was not there. His room was one of several on the first floor of the house. He glimpsed the two of them in the corridor ahead of him and presumed they were going into the same room. Humph, so she is with Mark.

The next morning Louis was woken by a pigeon sitting on the window-sill cooing. Lying on his back in the morning light his mind meandered through the rooms of the Gallery. I love birds, they make beautiful subjects for paintings. Funny how few birds there are in the Gallery. There are Zeus as an eagle in the *Rape of Ganymede* and *Leda and the Swan* of course. There are landscapes and mystical scenes that take place outside, lots of skies, water, trees, but few birds. Oh, mustn't forget flowers, there are plenty of them. Surprisingly, nudes are not as common as the general public imagine.

Stretching his arms and yawning he spoke out loud 'Well, no one is going to bring me a cup of coffee so I had better go find one.' and he pushed aside the cover.

The dining room was now set for breakfast with trays of croissant, dishes of bacon, eggs, kedgeree and cereal laid out in a buffet. David stood peering into an empty bowl hung-over.

'No kippers?' enquired Louis.

David pulled a silver lid off a large serving dish to reveal a steaming heap of smoked fish. After a couple of cups of coffee, kippers and eggs, David and Louis were at last in a fit state to converse with each other.

'So David, How did you meet Agata and Mark?'

'Well, Mark works for us now. He brought expertise to the table, knowledge and skills that I do not possess. Cyber security is critical now days.'

'Ah, so he and Agata are important to you. I didn't really understand. I assumed they were just new acquaintances.'

'Mark is important if a somewhat left brain, you know what I mean. Agata, she is a force unto herself.'

Anna burst into the room full of enthusiasm unwelcome after so much alcohol the night before. 'Happy birthday David!' she hugged her husband.

Louis had entirely forgotten about his friend's anniversary but shook David's hand with as much vigour as he could. Moments later, Agata came in from the garden. 'David, Anna, come on, the game has started.'

A littlie reluctantly David followed the two women out into the garden. Louis relieved at having been left alone helped himself to more kippers. Agata, returned with a smile. She paused and looked Louis in the eye, 'Come on, you must join us as my special guest. We're going to play croquet.' She held out her hand. Louis placed his trembling fingers on hers and she led him out to the lawn.

'Who invited him?' said Mark

'I did', said Agata, smiling, confident.

www.nationalgallery.org.uk/paintings/damiano-mazza-the-rape-of-ganymede
www.nationalgallery.org.uk/paintings/after-michelangelo-leda-and-the-swan

From that moment on Louis ceased to care what Mark or anyone else thought about him and his darling Agata. He was enchanted. More importantly, he was invited. Agata had expressly invited him to be with her.

Louis played along, as did everyone else. The only person who seemed to actually enjoy the game was Agata. But everyone made an effort. Just after noon, Agata finally yawned and looked at her phone for the time. She said, 'Oh my, I think last night is beginning to catch up with me. Maybe it's time for a lie down before lunch. What to you think Mark?'

'Yes darling, a pre-siesta siesta, perfect idea,' he replied.

They all headed to their bedrooms for a much-needed nap. Louis followed behind Agata and Mark again, but sober this time, he paused as he reached his room and noticed that they went into two separate rooms adjacent to each other. He pushed the door open and flopped on the bed. My goodness, she's not sleeping with him after all. He smiled and lay on his back with his hands behind his head.

He dosed off for a few minutes but was woken by a tap tap in the corridor. He stood up, creaked open his door and peered up the hallway. Giles was standing there as Agata greeted him, 'Giles, come on in,' she said as her arm came out and pulled Giles into her room by the waist and quickly closed the door.

Agata with Giles, what's going on? He went to his window which looked out onto the lawn strewn with croquet hoops and opened it. He leant out and strained to listen. Sure enough, her window was open and he just could just hear Agata's laugh and animated talking. A feeling of uncertainty engulfed him as if his life was now threatened. He sat on the bed and rubbed his chin. Either she's having it off with everyone or no one. I wonder which it is.

At one thirty lunch was announced with a gong. Louis heard doors open and people make their way from their rooms out to the veranda for another round of communal feasting. He looked out his window and saw Mark on the lawn smoking a cigarette. Agata's door opened and he heard her and Giles walk down the hall and stairs.

He followed them but continued on past the veranda into the garden to where Mark was taking a long drag. 'Want one Louis?' he said.

'Oh no, but thanks, I've never smoked cigarettes.'

Mark shrugged, looked at his shoes and took another drag.

'So how long have you and Agata known each other Mark?'

'Not long, about three months. My parents are Polish, although I was brought up in London. I guess we hit it off right away. We have a lot of things in common.'

'Have you spent much time in Poland?'

'Only when I was in the army. I was mostly in Germany, but I used to visit a lot.'

'The army?'

'Yeah, you know how it goes. Straight out of school, it was more like an apprenticeship.'

'Are you out of the army now?'

'Oh yes, it's a young mans game you know. We're all sent out to pasture before we become old and decrepit. I did get a medal from the Queen though.'

'David said you are in business together now.'

'Well, I look after security for the firm.'

Agata called out, 'Come on you two, champagne!'

Mark stubbed his cigarette into the lawn and they went back to the veranda. Louis found a seat at the far end of the table from Agata, Mark and Giles. Puzzled by their relationship to each other he quietly watched and listened to them. The three of them talked earnestly together all afternoon. But all the same, occasionally, Louis caught Agata looking at him with her piercing eyes.

Intrigued by her now and not a little frightened of Mark, he could not square him with Agata at all. Mark and Agata have a lot in common? They don't have anything in common. She's a PhD and he's a squadie. Perhaps Agata was just looking for friends when she arrived in London, any harbour in a storm. But whatever it was they had or have it won't last. What about Giles? He's a buffoon, a Hooray Henry. No Louis assured himself. Someone is going to end up with Agata, but it's not going to be Mark or Giles.

The rest of the day was a blur of champagne and brandy with birthday cake and a conga line through the garden after midnight. On Monday morning, Louis had no recollection of how or when he made it to bed. However he woke up as normal, his clothes neatly folded on the bedside chair.

Driving back to London he found a piece of paper in his pocket. He now remembered exchanging email addresses with Agata before going to bed and his heart pounded with excitement. Turning up the radio and increasing his speed, he drove straight home back to his beautiful family.

3

The next day Louis looked up the website for the Serpentine Gallery. The current exhibition was a series of nightmarish drawings of dogs wearing highly coloured knitted sweaters by an artist called Golub Leonus. Good grief, she can't possibly want to see this. He wrote an email to Agata.

> Hi Agata, It was very nice to meet you on the weekend. The Serpentine is showing an exhibition of Golub Leonus. Is that the one you were interested to see? In any case, if you ever need a tour guide for the National Gallery I would be happy to show you around.
> Take care,
> Louis

He took his time to review it before sending, his finger hovered over the mouse button. He didn't want to come on too strong, rather he thought, it's best to underplay it. Just send her something she can respond to, and then we can have an online conversation to get things going. He wanted to invite her out, but if she said no, then that would be the end of it. So instead he included a semi invitation that could be taken either way, open-ended. Satisfied, he clicked the send button and tried to forget about Agata until he received a reply.

Fortunately, the remainder of the week was taken up by a series of planning meetings. During breaks, he hurried back to his office to check his email. Friday afternoon came around, but he had received nothing from Agata. Disappointed he picked up his book and walked across Trafalgar Square to the Charring Cross tube and home.

The following Monday at work was peaceful. Far too peaceful and Louis clicked his send/receive button constantly hoping for a reply from Agata to suddenly appear. On Tuesday, he was beginning to give up hope until, a little tab from his email popped up - message received. His finger fumbled the mouse as he opened it.

> Louis! The days are flying by. I intended to drop you a line sooner, but a paper I'm writing has taken up all my free time. I have to go to Charring Cross Road near the National Gallery for an appointment tomorrow afternoon. I only have an hour to spare, but perhaps you could take me on the tour you mentioned? I guess you are going to the party this weekend? Hope to see you there.
> Agata.

He read the email over and over again. Slowly he typed a short reply. Seconds later he had a date with Agata from 2-3pm on the next day.

In the morning he left home with a spring in his step. He forgot his book and didn't notice anyone on the train. He flew up the steps of the gallery jauntily and said a merry hello to all the staff, his left hand not in his pocket, but waving by his side. Emily gave him a peculiar look as he said, 'Emily delightful morning isn't it?' with a beaming smile on his face.

He sat in his office without moving until five minutes to two. Then he pushed out into the stream of people and made his way to the Espresso Bar. It was a good place to meet people who were unfamiliar with the gallery as it's small and well sign posted. He stood at the entrance and at exactly two o'clock Agata walked up and smiled.

'Agata, how good to see you, would you like coffee?'

'No thanks Louis, too many already today.'

'Alright, well let's begin the tour, come with me.'

Louis put on his best professional air, which came naturally to him as he had taken hundreds of people through the gallery over the years, including his wife when she first visited him in London. 'The collection has over 2,300 works, with many priceless paintings including Velázquez's *Toilet of Venus* and Van Gogh's *Sunflowers*. We'll have a look at these, but let's start with Titian.'

www.nationalgallery.org.uk/paintings/

With his left hand in his jacket pocket, he led Agata up the stairs, through the Central Hall into room 2 and stopped in front of Titian's *Bacchus and Ariadne.*

He Began, 'Paintings at that time often told an elaborate story. Nowadays we are more used to narratives being unfolded in moving images with sound, or by reading. In the past people were more comfortable than we are today at seeing a whole story in a static painting. This one tells the story, in a poetic way, of Ariadne and the wine god Bacchus who fell in love with her at first sight.'

He took his left hand out of his pocket and pointed at Bacchus, 'Notice the stars in the sky above Ariadne...'

He glanced at Agata and realised that she was looking at his left hand and his wedding ring. Louis closed his fingers and put his hand back in his pocket. He felt his wedding ring and rolled it round and round. 'It's just a sentimental thing that's all,' he murmured unable to look at Agata.

Flustered he continued on as best he was able. Usually, he could talk endlessly about all the paintings in the gallery, but now his confidence was gone and in a perfunctory manner he led her from room to room fumbling his words all the way. They looked at *The Madonna of the Pinks*, by Raphael, Leonardo's Cartoon, paintings by Vermeer, Velázquez, van Gogh.

When they reached the rooms with the impressionists and post-impressionists, Agata became more interested. They paused for a long time at *After the Bath*, by Degas.

'Late in his career Degas began to draw women bathing and combing their hair. This one is a drawing of a woman sitting on a chair beside a bathtub, drying herself with a towel. Do you like it Agata?'

'Yes, this is my favorite so far. Somehow it is the most intimate. So many of the others we have looked at seem over staged, too well thought out perhaps.'

'Degas was famous for his meticulous composition and planning, but he more than likely watched this woman take a bath and then did an initial sketch which gives it a feeling of spontaneity.'

'I wonder what they talked about while she was bathing.'

'I don't know, but you can see how much he loves her form, her skin. It's sumptuous, full of texture and blurred lines that give a sense of movement.'

'Do you think he made love with this woman?'

'Perhaps, although probably not. He was intensely professional about

www.nationalgallery.org.uk/paintings/hilaire-germain-edgar-degas-after-the-bath-

his work. I think like all of the artists we have seen today, what he most loved was the beauty of the form, light, colour. Somehow they wanted to capture something of the vibrancy of life.'

'Capture it, own it,' she said with a bitter note to her voice.

'I think not in that sense, more that they wanted to preserve the moment, somehow keep the scene. Life is transient, fleeting. We all suffer the ravages of time, nothing lasts. I think they were trying to hold on to life.'

'I think that's where my interest in physics came from, a wish to understand the transience of the world, to piece together the history of life.'

'Isn't physics about the non-living world?'

'No, physics is the living world. The universe is made of matter, things, stuff. It is the way matter interacts, its elemental particles and the interrelationships between everything else that is the living world. Like a spider's web, pull a thread on the farthest edge and the vibrations are felt all across the weave.'

'And God is the spider?''

'Ah, God, that is something outside of my field,' she smiled.

'I think that artists, all artists throughout the ages are trying to put their finger on God, to stop God from moving around, to freeze God so we can say for sure that it's real.'

'That is an interesting idea, similar to quantum mechanics where objects only exist in a haze of probability. They have a certain chance of being at point A, another chance of being at point B and so on. You can't put your finger on it, stop it from moving. One instant it could be a wave, the next a particle or nothing at all.'

'So you don't discount the existence of God?'

'No, why should I. Our understanding of the universe is incomplete. We are like kindergarten children; we know practically nothing about the universe or existence.'

'Ah, what about the wisdom of eastern mysticism, philosophy, religion? Perhaps human knowledge is greater than the modern world acknowledges.'

'I am more interested in the real world, the one we live in rather than the one we imagine.'

'You're an existentialist! But is not the world we live in - the human condition - our collective imagination?'

'I'm not really an existentialist. I do expect that there are underlying universal principles to the structure to the universe. Perhaps we see the world from a unique viewpoint and that is who we are. But we exist now, here and that is what we must deal with. But you are a romantic I think?'

'Maybe I am a romantic, stuck in the nineteenth century. I do believe that the most important thing for an artist is to express their feelings, and not be bound by artificial rules.'

They moved on to the next room and the *Bathers at Asnières*, by Georges Seurat.

'This one is more like applied science, he seems to have defined the shapes by light alone. Somehow it doesn't seem painted,' said Agata.

'Yes, it is interesting the way he depicts the effects of light and atmosphere. Do you like this one?'

'I'm not sure, it gives a very vibrant effect, but the people...'

'I think he was after simplicity of form. The people in the painting, they are together sitting by the river, or bathing in it. It's a communal scene...'

'Yet they are not looking at each other. Their eyes are hidden from each other and us the viewers. It's a strange painting.'

'Your eyes, I mean, the way you look at me with your lovely eyes. Most paintings of people don't show the subject looking at the viewer. Sometimes they gaze into the distance,' said Louis.

'Mostly people don't look you in the eye, they are afraid. They don't want to give too much away.'

'But you look me in the eye Agata as if you can see into my heart.'

'I always look people in the eye.'

'Do you like what you see?'

'You look nice, interesting, but I can't really see into your heart.'

'Oh, the way you looked at me I thought you might find me attractive.'

'Looks aren't what make me want to be with a man. It's a spark about them, some sensibility that reaches me.'

'Do I have a spark?'

'Maybe, but you are so reserved it makes it hard for me to see the man behind the mask. What about your likes, what attracts you to a woman?'

'It's the same for me I think. There has to be a certain something, almost indefinable, the qualities you see in some of the great paintings, Rubens, Raphael, Leonardo and Picasso.'

'Wow, what high standards you have!'

'I don't mean they have to be a great beauty, it's the subtle quality that somehow the artist captures in time and space that lives on, their essence.'

www.nationalgallery.org.uk/paintings/georges-seurat-bathers-at-asnieres

'For you are paintings a substitute for real life? They are things in the past gone. No vibration on the spider's web will reach the women you see in paintings. I'm flesh and blood, real, alive. You can't love an ideal, an essence. You must love a person. Their good points bad points, the woman.'

'You want me to love you?'

'We were talking about art Louis.'

'Are you in love with someone?'

'Maybe, maybe not, that's personal, for me and the one I love.'

'Agata, you and Mark, are you?'

'No, no we're not. He has it in his head that I love him. I like him as a friend, but he has become a bit obsessed with me, that's all. I always seem to be surrounded by crazy people.'

'What about Giles?'

'Oh Giles, don't be silly. He's just a friend like you are Louis. We're friends aren't we?'

She looked at him with the hint of a tear in her eye. She peered into his eyes and he moved his face towards hers. She turned away and said, 'I have to go to my appointment now. Three o'clock, I'm already late.'

She walked towards the doorway, half turned and waved goodbye.

Louis looked at the Seurat and felt that he like the painting was stuck in time. She had gone and left him in a state of suspension.

He neglected to ask her about the party and he had no idea whose it was or where it was going to be. Ah ha, David will know. He called David while walking back to his office.

'David, we haven't spoken since your party. It was a fun weekend.'

'All a bit of a blur for me I'm afraid. I vaguely remember a conga line and a game of croquet, ' David replied.

'I must say that the weekend was a tonic for me. I haven't been socially active for years as you know. I got a bit of a taste for parties in fact. I don't suppose there is anything happening this weekend?'

'Louis, you're wondering if there is a party this weekend?'

'Just wondering, in case there is, you know...'

'You want to go a party? Funnily enough, there is a party this weekend.'

'Oh really, where?'

'Belgravia, you remember Giles? He was at my birthday. Anyway, he is having a do on Saturday night. Do you want to come with me?'

'If it's OK if I meet you there? I'll have to see when I can get away from the family. You know, pop out for an hour or so.'

'Right, 53 Chester Square, see you there.'

4

O n Saturday evening, he waited until Sandrine had gone to bed, snuck out of the apartment and took the tube from Bayswater to Sloane Square. As he walked the short distance to Chester Square, his nerves began to fray. What am I going to say to everyone? What will David think? He knows I don't go to parties. As soon as he sees me with Agata he'll know what's happening. In fact, I'm sure he had figured it out before he hung up the phone. What a fool I am.

Regardless, I think Agata wants me. This might be just my wild imagination, but I can tell that she feels for me. No I can't! I haven't the foggiest idea whether she fancies me or not. I can't divine her thoughts. All I know is how women look in paintings, their eyes turning inwards expressing something that neither I nor anyone else will ever grasp. But I can't let this go on past this night. I must find out tonight, one way or another, does she desire me or not? He walked with his hands stuffed into his pockets and his shoulders hunched. Almost involuntarily, he slipped his wedding ring off his finger and left it loose in his pocket.

As soon as Louis turned into the leafy square he could hear laughter and clinking glasses. One of the five-story terraces was ablaze with lights and people were visible through the windows that were open to the warm summer air. He pushed his way past a couple smoking on the front porch and through the front door. He helped himself to a glass of wine from a drinks table in the front room.

Looking for Agata, he went down the stairs to the basement and walked along the hallway. He grasped the edge of an open doorway and turned his head into a brightly lit room. Radiant, happy, holding forth, Agata was sitting on a sofa with Giles and David.

A pang of uncontrollable fear took hold of him. Stepping backward into the shadow of the hallway he felt unable to move fighting his instinct to flee. He could not bear the thought of facing David and Giles. Agata, framed by the open doorway tossed her head back in a laugh. He withdrew into himself unsure.

After a few moments, calmness came over him. Agata was talking and waving her hands, her eyes full of passion. Seeing only her, he stepped out into the light. She looked in his direction, and a smile moved across her face as their eyes met.

Louis walked into the room and reaching her looked down at her upturned face, he pushed his hand forward towards her's and Agata moved her fingers into his. He enclosed them and pulled at her hand. She stood up, and their lips embraced. Without speaking, he led her out of the room and up the stairs.

They pushed past a group of people sitting on the steps. Louis held her hand firmly and they continued up until they arrived at the top floor. Looking down the corridor he saw an empty bedroom with no light on but the door ajar. He led her inside and closed the door behind them. In the darkness without speaking they embraced, kissed, and Louis cupped her breast.

Seconds later a loud knock on the door startled them. Their eyes were adjusting to the darkness with light spreading in from the window. Louis looked at Agata and motioned her to stand aside out of view while he opened the door.

Mark, his face red demanded, 'Is Agata with you? She was seen coming up here.'

'No Mark, look, I'm just a bit dizzy, drunk and I need to lie down for a moment,' and he closed the door with a bang. Mark stamped on the floor outside and shuffled his feet noisily, 'Agata, come out for fucks sake.'

Louis moved Agata towards the bed and motioned her to sit down. He whispered in her ear, 'Do you want to go with him?'

'No,' she said shaking her head.

'Is he your lover?'

'No, I told you, he's obsessed with me, I can't shake him.'

He held her hand and kissed her moist lips. He felt sure now, she did want him and he would abandon everything for her, surrender himself to her. He moved her to lie down. Taught she pressed her body to his as if afraid to let go. They kissed but after a few moments she inched her face away from his and resisted his hands, uncertain now.

That idiot Mark interrupted the perfect moment; she was going to give herself to me, thought Louis. He changed tack and began to whisper sweet nothings softly in her ear. 'It was your eyes, the way you looked at me, I knew you wanted me, you do want me, you know it, let yourself go. Everything will be alright. I feel so much for you, darling...'

'Yes, but you are married, she said,'

Their hands entwined she searched his fingers for his ring. When she didn't feel it, she withdrew back into herself a little more. 'You're a liar, she whispered.'

'I'm not, I like you a lot, I don't know where it's all going, but we have tonight, let's follow our passion.'

'Sometimes you wear a wedding ring, sometimes not, you're a liar.'

'Don't worry about my stupid ring, sentimental that's all, I told you.'

'So where is your wife?'

'Forget about her, she's away, she went home, that's that.'

'Just for a few weeks.'

'No, no, months. What can I do, what can I say. I'm here with you. I didn't plan to fall for you, nor you me.'

'I like you Louis, you're interesting, we can just be friends.'

'You can never be friends with one that you desire, or who desires you.'

'Oh, so some friend you are blackmailing me.'

'No, I'm just saying, it's true, afterwards, after a couple make love, then they're intimate and can be friends. Until then it is impossible no matter how much they like each other, all their being is full of tension, unfulfilled desire.'

'So you're saying that we can never be friends because we are attracted to each other, but we have to make love so we can become friends?'

'Yes, it's an illogical, unreasonable situation. So what are we to do? I think that as we want each other we should make love, and take it from there.'

'We can't just make love here, in someone else's room with Mark prowling around.'

'Then come away with me, we can leave right now.'

'Louis, don't be ridiculous, you have a wife and I have my life here I can't just run away with you.'

'Just for a few days, so we can get to know each other and see where this goes. Come with me right now. We can spend the night at the Cadogan Hotel a short walk from here. Tomorrow we'll take the train to Paris and stay at the Pavillon de la Reine, for just a few days then we'll see.'

'Those hotels sound expensive.'

'They are, very expensive indeed. The Pavillion is an exquisite hotel in the best part of Paris where all the highest class Haute couture and jewellery shops are. The hotel restaurant is world famous. Of course, we'll also have the whole of Paris to enjoy. We'll have a fabulous, romantic time. '

'I have to work on Monday.'

'You can take a few days off, personal reasons, they won't mind.'

'Saying personal reasons is better than sick as that would be untrue.'

'Exactly, so it will be fine. Come on let's go, now.'

'Do you know Paris well?'

'Yes, nearly as well as I know London. My mother is from Paris.'

'Oh, so that's where you got the name Louis.'

'Yes, I'm named after my Grandfather, not King Louis don't worry. I can show you all the secret romantic places in Paris. Places tourists never see.'

'You know, I've not been to Paris. I went straight from university in Warsaw to post graduate studies at Harvard. I'm more at home in the USA than in Europe.'

'I can't wait to hear all about it, darling. But I don't hear Mark outside anymore. So let's stand up now and we can walk to the Cadogan. Isn't this exciting?'

He stood up and pulled her arm to lift her off the bed, but she resisted. She pulled his hand back and made him lie next to her again. They lay in silence. Louis moved his lips to her earlobe and kissed her. He whispered, 'Agata, we didn't plan this. I just walked into David's house and there you were. I had no idea I was going to meet you, fall for you. But I did meet you and I know you fell for me.'

'I'm falling alright, but no Louis, I can't go away with you. You can never be serious with me, you have a wife.'

'You don't know my situation. I'm free to be with you, and here we are tonight, together, full of desire, we will never be here again, open up, take me, now, tonight.'

'Louis, I hear you, but if this is real it will last a bit of time. I need to think, to reflect on what you've said. Let me think it over. I must go now.'

'Agata, just relax and wait a while. There's no hurry, we can keep talking.'

She pushed her arm against the bed to stand up, but Louis resisted and gently stopped her. Her eyes tightened, angry now.

'Stay, stay with me now, I won't do anything, just lie down and keep talking to me.'

'You won't do anything, sure. No, I'm going now.'

'Agata, this is our night, here we are together now, hold me close, stay with me.'

'So you don't care about your wife?'

'Of course I do, but I care more about you, us. Don't worry about my wife, she's not in the frame any more. It's something I have to sort out. I want to be with you.'

Agata stood up, resolute, and moved towards the door. Turning to look at him, she said, 'We can talk again tomorrow.'

'Agata, tonight belongs to us, try and understand. Will you come away with me?'

'Maybe I'll go to Paris with you, give me tonight to think about it.'

Agata closed the door behind her leaving Louis as if in a vacuum, in space, alone.

He lay on the bed, mon Dieu, he thought, I wasn't wrong, she does want me, she does. He was elated, but a sense of failure enveloped him. He opened the door and made his way quickly down the stairs and walked straight out the front door of the house. He bumped into Mark who was smoking a cigarette and nearly knocked him over.

'Mark, so sorry I didn't see you.'

'It's alright Louis, where's Agata?'

'I just have to make a call, I'll be back soon.'

'Where is she?' he shouted after him.

Louis walked as briskly as he could to the corner of the square and turned left into Eccleston Street. He barely stopped, even for traffic until he reached the safety of home. His wife was asleep as he crept into bed. He reached out to touch her, but pulled his hand back. Curling himself into a ball, he gathered the covers over his head and closed his eyes.

5

The next morning he awoke to the sound of his baby crying. Sandrine came into the room and picked up petite Julie and carried her downstairs. Mysterious, Sandrine is, with her unknowable smile, like the most famous painting in the world. Maybe that is her uniqueness. What goes on inside her head, her heart? I see so much in her face, but I don't know if what I see is real, correct. I don't know what her desires are, except to work, raise our daughter and love me too. Is that enough, all? I don't think I have ever understood.

He turned over to lie down again and the memory of the night before returned. Agata, oh my, how could you slip my mind even for a moment? My flirtation is over, thank goodness. Yes she does desire me, that's all I needed to know. But why did she pull away from me? How could I be so near, so close to her but fail to win her?

He pulled himself out of bed and went downstairs for breakfast. Glancing at the kitchen clock he saw it was late, he had slept in.

Agata said she would think about my proposal and we would talk again today. What if she calls me? She doesn't have my number. David might give it to her, what if Sandrine answers? David won't give her the landline stupid! Still, I had better call her.

Louis didn't have Agata's phone number, just her email address. He logged into his email and found her message to him and was relieved that she had included her number at the bottom. He couldn't call her from home so he put on his jacket and opened the front door. 'Darling, I'll be back soon,' he shouted to Sandrine.

He walked around the corner to Moscow Road and the Byzantium Cafe and sat down at a table. 'Espresso please,' he called to the waitress.

What am I going to say to Agata? Fear crept over him like a chill wind. I failed last night, mercifully. What if she had said yes and we had just woken up at the Cadogan? I would be calling a cab to go to St Pancras station to catch the Eurostar to Paris. On the way there I would have to call the Pavillon de la Reine to make a reservation. That hotel costs an absolute fortune! My god, I would be paying off my credit card for the next ten years. Do I even have enough credit for one night there? What was I thinking? He felt desperate for a cigarette even though he had never smoked in his life.

His coffee arrived and he put a lump of sugar in and stirred it with his teaspoon, then another lump, then another, stirring vigorously. 'Would you like some coffee with your sugar, love?' the waitress laughed.

Louis picked up his tiny cup and threw the viscous lukewarm liquid in the back of his throat. His fingers began tapping the table like playing drums. I haven't done that since I was twelve. He remembered his mother chiding him as if he were a digging with a jackhammer, 'Arrête le marteau pneumatique garçon méchant!'

The coffee helped to calm him down and his thoughts began to coalesce. OK, she'll decide no and that will be that. What if she says yes? She won't, she's not stupid. She must know I'm mad. She'll think that I'd say anything to get her into bed, and of course she's right. That fool Mark, if only he hadn't come looking for her like a lunatic, I would be in bliss, right now, with Agata in my arms!

He stood up and paced around the cafe. The waitress looked at him nervously and the only other customer left hurriedly. 'Are you alright sir?' she asked.

'Schhh, I'm thinking,' he barked.

He sat back down. Bliss, agony, bliss agony, either way there would have been much agony. I could not have stayed with Agata. I would have hurt her, hurt Sandrine, hurt myself. But I would have risked it all to be with her, I would have done it, I would be on that train now. Who knows where I would have ended up?

He reached for his phone in his jacket pocket but felt his wedding ring instead. He slipped it back on his finger and found the phone in his other pocket.

'Hi, it's Louis, how are you today?'

'Louis, I'm OK I guess.'

'How is Mark?'

'Mark? Oh, I don't know I haven't seen him.'

'It's just, you know, he was looking for you.'

'Yes, he kept looking for me alright.'

'He did? Oh, crikey, well um...'

'All the men I know seem to be unhinged, don't worry I'm used to it.'

'Well I'll never act crazy, I promise you that.'

'You, not act crazy?'

Louis paused, and asked, 'Are we OK, Agata, you and I?'

'Yeah, sure, no problem with me.'

Louis felt unease in Agata that he was not expecting, 'Agata what are your plans for today?'

'Well, I don't know, you suggested a lot of things last night, but I don't really know you, so you know ...'

'Ah well, I understand, of course, you don't know me it's true.'

'So I don't know, I can't just, you know...'

'No, no of course not, it was silly of me to think, no, needless to say, I understand. So, enjoy the rest of your weekend.'

'Oh, alright then Louis, of course we can still go to the Serpentine I suppose?'

'The Serpentine, of course, call me whenever you want to go I'd love that, sure. So, goodbye now.'

'OK, goodbye.'

Once again, Louis asked himself, what just happened? Did I ditch her or did she ditch me? I hope it was she that ended it because hell hath no fury as that of a woman scorned.

Uncertain, as if something was missing, he still felt relieved. So did the waitress when he paid for his coffee and left. He went home to his beautiful wife and lovely baby and acted as if nothing had ever happened, except, that during the day a feeling of heaviness and loss came over him.

Holding his baby distracted him, but when he put her down, the memory of Agata's eyes came back to him. What did she mean when she said, '... he kept looking for me alright.' Did Mark eventually find her? I was not terribly brave. I didn't make sure she got home, just left the party.

What did she mean when she said, 'You, not act crazy?' So she thought my insane pleading was crazed? She really does know what an idiot I am! She seemed pensive, uneasy. No, I know now, she wanted me to take her to Paris, that's it. Last night I was so ardent, and today I backed off completely. I made no effort to persuade her, I didn't even have any words of love for her. So she does feel scorned. She does think it was me who dumped her.

Oh no, what will she do now? I spurned her, she hates me,. She demurred and went home not prepared to give in so easily, but was eager and waiting for me to continue my advances and what happened? The coward I am, I ran away.

Louis hands and shoulders began shuddering. He lay down on the bed feeling ill in his stomach. What will she do to me now? She'll denounce me for sure. She'll say terrible things against me. I'll lose my wife, my baby, my career, I'm destroyed.

On Monday, he ran up the steps of the gallery. He forgot to nod good morning to the staff. He hurried into his office without even noticing lovely Emily. His swagger was gone with his left hand flapping like a rope dangling in the wind. Distracted, he put off returning phone calls and emails. After lunch, he sat down again at his computer and wrote to Agata.

> Agata, it was nice to see you at the weekend. I am
> looking forward to going to the Serpentine Gallery with
> you. Let me know when you want to go. Best, L

Louis read the email before sending it. He wanted to let her know that he had not actually dumped her but was still interested in her. Humm, nothing controversial there, click, he sent it.

He waited nervously all week, desperate for a reply. If only she would respond and let me off the hook. Why does she torture me like this? Please email me so I know everything will be alright. We can have a coffee and a chat and be friends. But nothing ever came.

The weekend arrived and Louis moped around the house. Sandrine became worried about him, 'Are you ill cheri?'

'I'm fine, just tired after a hard week nothing more.'

Wild scenarios engulfed him. He could think of nothing except how Agata could hurt him, but surely she won't? If only she would reply to my email with a kind word he lamented. He imagined her talking to David, '... he's not just married, he has a four-month-old baby.'

What on earth must she think of me? She'll set Mark onto me, a soldier, security. Oh my, he was probably SAS, why else would he have received a medal from the Queen? He imagined innumerable ways that Agata would take her revenge upon him, with Mark as her henchman.

Back at work on Monday, he sat tapping his desk with his fingers. I cannot write another email to Agata. If she hasn't replied to the first one, I must not write to her again. He was determined to keep his dignity and not act in desperation. 'Damn it!' he shouted reaching for his keyboard.

> Agata, I hope that you and Mark are going along
> well? Let me know, I would love to hear your news.
> Coffee, exhibition? Whenever you're free. Louis

To hell with it, click, sent.

As the week progressed, his composure gradually returned, as much from exhaustion as anything else. On Friday afternoon just as he was about to leave for the weekend - message received - popped onto his screen.

> Louis, let's go the Serpentine Gallery tomorrow if
> you are free. A
> Agata, OK but meet me at the Serpentine Bar &
> Kitchen at the end of the lake. We can have a coffee
> before the exhibition. Is noon OK with you? L

He couldn't bear the thought of going to the Golub Leonus exhibition. A soon as he sent the reply he thought, why did I say noon? I'll never hold out until then. I should have said ten or nine. In any case, he now had an appointment with Agata. At last he could relax a bit. He went home feeling as if he had been through a wringer every day for the last two weeks.

He arrived at the Serpentine Kitchen at eleven o'clock. He could not pace up and down his living room any longer without increasing Sandrine's already deep suspicion. He found a table outside on the terrace with a view over the lake and ordered an espresso.

There were many ducks and geese paddling in the water. Fisherman on the bank lounged back in their chairs waiting for a bite. It was a warm day and bathers lolled about in the water of Lido swimming area and sunbathed on the shore. A slight breeze made small ripples on the water. Puffy white clouds floated overhead creating shadow, dappled light then brilliant sunshine and back to shadow. The scene was reminiscent of the Seurat, *Bathers at Asnières*, in the Gallery. He dozed off in the sunshine and Agata startled him when she arrived.

'Louis Louis!' she raised her voice as she sat down.

'Agata, how nice to see you, I arrived a while ago and was enjoying the view.'

'It's beautiful. I have not been here before, so peaceful.'

'How have you been Agata?'

'Busy, you know. Sorry I didn't get back to you sooner. To be honest, I didn't know what to say to you.'

'Are you mad at me?'

'Mad at you, no. I wonder about you though. What you are about, what you were thinking.'

'I don't believe there was any logical thought behind my actions or words actually. It all came from my Gallic heart.'

'The things you said to me, then you brushed me aside.'

'Did I? I didn't mean to. I became frightened I think.'

'Frightened of me?'

'I was frightened of the situation, frightened for myself in truth.'

'Ah, at last, some honesty from you.'

'Was I so dishonest with you?'

'It was hard for me to think that you really cared about me at all.'

'That is the one thing that is true Agata, I fell for you, I was afraid to say it to you, but I felt love for you. I would have gone all the way for you.'

'But only for a few hours, then you would have returned home to your, family, your baby.'

'No, no, not just a few hours. I would have given everything for you.'

'Everything? That would not have been right. What do you think I am? I don't want to ruin you life.'

'Why did you, I mean, you knew that I was married, why did you let me get close to you?'

'I don't know Louis, I liked you. I just followed my heart, or maybe it was my body. I was attracted to you. I felt something for you, but I realised too late that you are taken already.'

'When did you find out about my baby?'

'I hadn't asked David about you before, but I felt a bit despondent after you hung up and I called him. We met later in the day.'

'I guess I pre-empted your answer. I never found out what you would have said. Would you have gone to Paris with me?'

'When you called I didn't know what I would say. I expected more from you. Maybe I would have gone away with you, but you seemed to have changed your mind. Now I know, you were only playing with me.'

'I wasn't playing with you. I'm not used to the attention of a beautiful woman like you. I didn't know how to behave.'

'You seem so sophisticated as if you are in control.'

'It's all a disguise I'm sorry to say. Underneath I'm a writhing mess of fear and inadequacy.'

'I'm the same, I assure you.'

'I keep asking, but what about Mark? Did you see him that night after you left me in the room?'

'Yes, yes he found me downstairs. We had an argument, it was horrible.'

'I'm sorry, I feel a coward. I should have done something.'

'Oh, it's alright it wasn't your fault. I hate anything clinging to me and he tries to suffocate me. Ever since I left Poland, I've met nothing but psychotic men.'

'That's a bit strong, regarding me at least, I think.'

'Well, neurotic then. It was the same in America. I met guys who wanted too much, too little or were just too weird. That was one of the reasons I took the job in London. I would like to meet someone special, someone to care for me. Since I arrived, there was Mark. He was nice at first. But then he became so possessive, following me, checking up on me even after I broke it off with him. Then Giles, who's like a little child. He needs a mother, not a lover. David is different ...'

'David no?'

'At least it's not complicated with him. He only wants one thing and is quite up front about it.'

'Of course, I suppose it makes sense.'

'Then there is you Louis. What can I say about you?'

'That you forgive me, that you still like me.'

'Oh I forgive you, don't worry. Maybe I should go back to Poland. There the men are normal at least.'

'We can be friends can't we Agata?'

'You're the one who said lovers can't be friends.'

'Actually, I said we couldn't be friends until we became lovers.'

'Well, we didn't become lovers, did we?'

'Apart from a few stolen kisses. Could we try again? I won't be so foolish this time.'

'No Louis, as you said we only had that one night. I think you just wanted to collect me, put me in your exhibition, hang me up.'

'I'm not like that Agata. I have no trophies.'

"No? Your wife is she not just part of your collection? If not how could you think of replacing her so easily?'

Louis lowered his face unable to answer. Had he wanted to replace Sandrine? Did David and Agata know him better than he knew himself? Perhaps they were the ones catagorising, sorting, putting people in pigeon holes, curating.

He watched a Canada goose as it paddled along the lake's edge. He raised his eyes, slowly. Like a canvas spread out before him, he gradually took in the whole scene attempting to divine the message the artist was trying to convey.

An old gentleman walked slowly down the lake shore towards the Lido with a cane and a boater hat. Two ladies, arm in arm strolled towards him bowing a greeting as they passed. Children splashed in the water while their parents looked on from the shore, talking amongst themselves. A young woman on a towel with a book was talking to a young man a short distance away sitting on his towel. A couple in rowboat stroked lazily along, talking and giggling. The breeze caught the full grown summer leaves in the trees which rustled distantly. The smell of cut lawn and roses filled the air in a sweet mix evocative of days gone by.

Such a civilised scene, he thought. Everyone was courteous, exchanging pleasantries, interested in each other. In the Seurat they were too introspective, only thinking about themselves. Not as Agata said, 'Like a spider's web, pull a thread on the farthest edge and the vibrations are felt all across the weave.' Louis looked around. Agata had gone, he was alone. He felt detached from the web. He couldn't feel its vibrations; only look from afar. Like a viewer, outside the frame.

****

Sean De Siun spent his early years in Australia before moving to London in the early 1970s.

His written works include non fiction redactions, documentaries, screenplays and short stories. He currently lives with his wife in Sydney Australia.

Also by the author and available
from Fileata Fiction

Kings Road
Caanice and the Book
Katie
Desire
Chatter

Copy Sales
The Curator is available on **www.amazon.com**
Purchase direct from **www.fileata.com**